MARK TWAIN
KING LEOPOLD'S SOLILOQUY

MARK TWAIN

KING LEOPOLD'S
SOLILOQUY

INTERNATIONAL PUBLISHERS
NEW YORK

© Seven Seas Books, 1961
Published simultaneously by
International Publishers, New York, and
Seven Seas Books, Berlin, 1970

This printing, 2006

ISBN 13: 978-0-7178-0687-4
ISBN 10: 0-7178-0687-1

Library of Congress CIP Data

Twain, Mark, 1835-1910
    King Leopold's soliloquy / Mark Twain
        p. cm.
    Reprint. Originally published: Boston, Mass. : P.R.
Warran, 1905
    ISBN 13: 978-07178-06874 $5.00
    ISBN 10: 07178-06871
    1. Leopold II, King of the Belgians, 1835-1909--Fiction
    2. Zaire--History--to 1908--Fiction   I. Title.
    PS1322.K5   1991
    813'.4--dc20

91-10670

    CIP

Briefly,

ABOUT THE BOOK

This is a rare book for a number of reasons. First, it is written by Mark Twain, second, it was buried in silence for more than a half century and third, few copies exist. This new edition gives today's readers the chance to get to know a work by a great man which would become lost to time ... The subject is as alive today as when it was written in 1905. For this is a story of the crime in the Congo, crime carried on by rod and by rood. Told with biting satire, and fired with the hate of injustice which made Mark Twain loved by the plain man and ridiculed by the cynic, this book is important reading for any one who wants to understand what is happening in Africa today. Illustrated with line drawings and with an introduction by Stefan Heym, this is indeed a rare book.

CONTENTS

*Introduction
by Stefan Heym*   11

King Leopold's Soliloquy   31

Supplementary   77

*Report of the
King's Commission*   80

*The United States
and the Congo State*   83

*Interview with
Rev. John H. Harris*   87

AN ORIGINAL MISTAKE

This work of "civilization" is an enormous and continual butchery. All the facts we brought forward in this chamber were denied at first most energetically; but later, little by little, they were proved by documents and by official texts. The practice of cutting off hands is said to be contrary to instructions; but you are content to say that indulgence must be shown and that this bad habit must be corrected "little by little" and you plead, moreover, that only the hands of *fallen* enemies are cut off, and that if hands are cut off "enemies" not quite dead, and who, after recovery, have had the bad taste to come to the missionaries and show them their stumps, it was due to an original mistake in thinking that they were dead. *From Debate in Belgian Parliament, 1903.*

INTRODUCTION

If after more than half a century a man's words still have the force of dynamite, you cannot call him a clown. They tried that in his lifetime; they tried to bury him under that caption for fifty years after his death; but Mark Twain the fighter refused to stay buried, and his pen, sharp and merciless, is still a weapon.

Mark Twain took seriously the writer's duty to be the conscience of his time. He risked fortune, success, the applause of the press and the favors of the government; he turned his humor into stinging satire; and the harder certain of his contemporaries attempted to type him a funny man, the angrier he became.

Yes, the man who made millions laugh was an angry man because he was a seeing man. He saw what went on in the world around him, and he refused to blind himself or encrust his heart with complacency. He saw who was enemy and who was friend; he sided with the Filipinos who were butchered by the U. S. Army; with the Chinese massacred by the troops of Russia's Czar and Germany's Kaiser, Britain's King and America's President; with the Negroes lynched by church-going, God-fearing white Southern hypocrites; and with the workers bled and exploited everywhere. He hit, and he hit hard; nor did he cringe when the stuff started flying.

He would have been invaluable for us today, for our fight. We could use Mark Twain's pen.

In fact, we do use it — now.

Mark Twain's pen rips a large, jagged tear into a blanket of silence. The men who ruled the Congo in Mark Twain's time liked silence — as do their successors of today. Such men operate best in the dark, and nothing disturbs them more than the sudden light of truth. That's why Mark Twain's political writings have largely been "forgotten"; that's why "King Leopold's Soliloquy" isn't contained in any edition of his works we know of and why this is the first reprint since the original publication, 1905, in Boston and, 1906, in England.

The conspiracy of silence began almost immediately after the book appeared. The impact of "King Leopold's Soliloquy" had been terrific. By December, 1905, Henry I. Kowalsky, one of the Belgian King's agents in the United States, reports to his boss of the strong anti-Leopold movement that has sprung up. "Monster petitions have been circulated and signed," he writes, "the industry of the opposition is very manifest, and I can assure you that you cannot afford to turn a deaf ear to what I am saying." And though every quip coming from Mark Twain made headlines in the American press, on this issue the newspapers remained silent. Their discretion becomes understandable when we learn that, in 1906, King Leopold permitted a few Americans to buy into his Congo business: Messrs. J. P. Morgan, John D. Rockefeller, Thomas Fortune Ryan, and Daniel Guggenheim. Their money has been in the Congo business ever since.

Mark Twain could hardly have been surprised at this. He knew the nature of the forces against whom he had arraigned himself. He was intensely aware of the changes in his country which the end of the nineteenth century had seen effected, In March, 1899, the *New York World* could report, "More industrial trusts and monopolistic 'combines' were formed in 1898 than in the entire quarter of a century since the Standard Oil Company, parent and pattern of American monopoly, first began to destroy competition in illuminating oil."

Along with monopoly came its grab for other lands, came imperialism. Mark Twain not only knew the term, he knew the workings of the thing, its essence. In his book "Following the Equator," published 1897, Twain writes, "In many countries we have chained the savage and starved him to death . . . in many countries we have burned the savage at the stake . . . we have hunted the savage and his little children and their mother with dogs and guns . . . in many countries we have taken the savage's land from him, and made him our slave, and lashed him every day, and broken his pride and made death his only friend, and overworked him till he dropped in his tracks . . ." And, "There are many humorous things in the world; among them the white man's notion that he is less savage than other savages."

Mark Twain knew imperialism. And he knew its corroding influence on democracy in America, on his own people. "Money is the supreme idea," he writes to his friend Twichell. "Money-lust has always existed, but not in the history of the world was it ever a craze, a madness, until your time and mine." And he adds that it has made his own America "hard, sordid, ungentle, dishonest, oppressive."

Mark Twain did not learn about imperialism from books. He knew Gorki and befriended him; but he did not know Lenin or Lenin's thoughts on the subject. Mark Twain observed certain trends and reached conclusions from what he saw. He traveled widely and noted imperialism in operation abroad; within the borders of his country he saw imperialism's reflection in the treatment of Chinese and Negroes.

And he heard the cant of imperialism, the verbiage which later on, almost word for word, he was to let drip from King Leopold's lips in the "Soliloquy." He heard President McKinley declaim, in 1899, to a delegation of Methodists, ". . . there was nothing left for us to do but to take them all, and to educate the Filipinos, and uplift and civilize and Christianize them, and by God's grace do the very best by them as our fellow-men for whom Christ also died."

So Mark Twain took his stand. "I am an anti-imperialist," he stated to the press. That was in the fall of 1900, upon his return to the United States. "I am opposed to having the eagle put his talons on any other land."

It seems strange, then, that in this book against Leopold of Belgium, one of the biggest brigands ever spawned by imperialism, Mark Twain never uses the word. Instead, he concentrates on the person, on the king: including the revelation of details of Leopold's private life. Had Twain forgotten the general truth over the horrors of the special case? Had he been carried away by that fascination with, and contempt for, nobility and royalty which bob up in his works, from "Huckleberry Finn" with its *Duke of Bilgewater* and *the wanderin', exiled, trampled-on, and sufferin' rightful King of France*, through "The American Claimant," "The Prince and the Pauper," "Joan of Arc," "A Connecticut Yankee in King Arthur's Court," and on to the two great soliloquies he wrote, the "Czar's" and "King Leopold's"?

Mark Twain, always a man of strong loves and hates, never lets emotion carry him away from the rules of his craft. "King Leopold's Soliloquy," though written at white heat, also shows the conscious use of structure, the proper dosage of ideas, the calculated effect of repetition, the relentless drive at the exact points the author wishes to make. Mark Twain the artist remains an artist even when a propagandist; Twain artfully chooses to flail King Leopold the individual, in the flesh, concrete, rather than some abstract ism, knowing that in hitting Leopold he strikes the straightest blow at the ism he hates.

Mark Twain didn't pick his target lightly. When in the fall of 1904, Mr. E. D. Morel, head of the Congo Reform Association in England, asked Mark Twain to lend his pen "for the cause of the Congo natives," the request reached a man ready and willing. On Thanksgiving Day of the same year, Mark Twain had let off steam with a piece he never published, entitled "A Thanksgiving Sentiment." His sentiment that day was, "We have much to be thankful for. Our free Republic being the official godfather of the Congo Graveyard; first of the Powers to recognize its pirate flag become responsible through silence for the prodigious depredations & multitudinous murders committed under it upon the helpless natives by King Leopold of Belgium in the past twenty years: now therefore let us be humbly thankful that this last twelve-month has seen the King's usual annual myriad of murders reduced by nearly one & one half per cent; let us be humbly grateful that the good King, our pet & protégé, due in hell these sixty-five years, is still spared to us to continue his work & ours among the friendless & the forsaken; & finally let us live in the blessed hope that when in the Last Great Day he is confronted with his unoffending millions upon millions of robbed, mutilated and massacred men, women & children, & required to explain, he will be as politely silent about us as we have been about him."

Throughout this bitter reflection disguised as a prayer runs the thread that later is to be woven into the whole of Twain's book on the subject, the thread that forever ties the crimes of the robber monarch who rules Belgium, to the robber barons who rule Mark Twain's own country, the United States.

Having chosen his target, Mark Twain proceeds to select the methods best suited to his attack. From his political pieces he takes the two with the hardest impact on people's minds, and combines their approaches. "In *Defense* of General Funston" and "The Czar's *Soliloquy*" are merged to become "King Leopold's *Soliloquy — A Defense* of his Congo Rule."

A man's soliloquy — a man's talking or thinking to himself — unmasks that man's inner being. Any dramatist, any novelist knows the trick and uses it time and again. Mark Twain uses it as a political hook and after "Bloody Sunday" in Moscow on January 22, 1905, he hangs on it that contemptible Czar and his entire contemptible, blood-drenched system, for the whole world to see and to despise.

A man's defense — a man's attempt to defend the indefensible — can condemn him more surely than a plea of guilty. Any prosecutor knows the trick and uses it time and again. Mark Twain uses this, too, as a political hook and hangs on it, in the year 1902, that able representative of early American imperialism, Frederick Funston, Brigadier-General of Volunteers in the American Army and captor, by low and scurvy treachery, of the Filipino leader Aguinaldo.

"In Defense of General Funston" as well as "The Czar's Soliloquy," individually and each for its purpose, had caused a furor. The combination of the two could be expected to pack a double blow.

Mark Twain's star witnesses and, simultaneously, the soliloquizing King's most annoying adversaries, are the missionaries — Protestant, Catholic, any old kind of missionaries — in the Congo.

To read this book, one might conclude Twain thought all missionaries in the colonies to be a sainted boon to the natives and their sole source of consolation and succor, and certainly his own most admired friends.

Actually, Twain had no illusions about the character and function of the missionaries. In 1896, one of his notebook jottings reads, "It is a most strange vocation, the missionary's... the religious deserter ranks with the military deserter; it is considered that he has done a base thing & shameful. It is the mish's trade to make religious deserters."

In his article "To the Person Sitting in Darkness," published in *The North American Review* of February, 1901, Twain goes further. He describes the missionaries as an integral part of what he calls the "Blessings-of-Civilization Trust" — imperialism — that deals in "Glass Beads and Theology, and Maxim Guns and Hymn Books, and Trade Gin and Torches of Progress and Enlightenment (patent adjustable ones, good to fire villages with, upon occasion)." In the introduction to the piece, Twain quotes a letter from the Rev. William Ament of the American Board of Foreign Missions, published in the *New York Sun*. In the letter, the diligent Reverend reports that he had collected damages of 300 taels each for one hundred Board-converted Chinese Christians who were killed during the Boxer uprising, that he had extracted full compensation payment for all Christian property destroyed, and finally had assessed fines to the Chinese villagers, totaling thirteen times the amount of the indemnity. The Rev. Ament justified this blackmail by saying that the money would be used "for the propagation of the Gospel" and by pointing out that his colleagues of the Catholic faith not only extorted 500 taels for each of their converts killed, but also demanded 680 heads for the 680 Catholic Chinese killed in Wenchiu district.

The idea of a monument of skulls, so lovingly described by Mark Twain in "King Leopold's Soliloquy," takes shape here, in connection with this gentle missionary. Ament's "magnanimity," writes Twain, should be commemorated by a monument with a design showing the thirteen-fold indemnity. The monument further should "exhibit 680 Heads, so disposed as to give a pleasing and pretty effect, for the Catholics have done nicely, and are entitled to notice in the monument."

The Christian missionary, teaching the native to accept his miserable lot on earth in return for *post mortem* rewards up above, supplies the ideology that goes with absolute submission to the colonial bosses. That's why he follows, a dutiful shadow, the strutting conquistador and the trader, the big planter and the policeman, the big exploiter and the whip-swinging overseer. But like any purveyor of ideology he often feels uncomfortable at the contradictions between the beliefs he has to peddle and reality, especially if his beliefs are in themselves as contradictory as those of Christianity. To preach, "Love Thy Neighbor," to people whose children's hands have just been hacked off by the very neighbors in question, might be hypocrisy too strong for even a missionary to stomach. The missionaries in this particular instance are not against colonialism, not against imperialism, not even against the rule of the Belgians in the Congo —they're just against King Leopold's methods.

But this is enough to turn them into Mark Twain's allies. Twain is far from sectarian fussiness. He takes his witnesses where he finds them. In fact, he has to take their testimony because there is no other. King Leopold has seen to it that aside from his own officials and henchmen, no one can enter his special preserve, the Congo Free State. No one, that is, except a British consul by the name of Roger Casement, and a few missionaries.

King Leopold's agent, Henry I. Kowalsky, was correct in decrying the effect on America of Mark Twain's book. The House of Morgan and the Rockefeller interests, freshly entered upon the Congo business, found it equally upsetting. Choking off all echo in the press seemed insufficient; mysterious sources financed an "Answer to Mark Twain," a pamphlet charging him with "infamous libel against the Congo State"; professors and clergymen, up to and including Cardinal Gibbons, were paid to defend the system by which the Congo was exploited.

A lot was at stake. Until now, the money in the Congo had been made on rubber and ivory. But in 1906, the year in which "King Leopold's Soliloquy" struck its blow, the Union Minière du Haut Katanga was founded. There was copper in the Congo's Katanga province, ores containing eight per cent of pure metal, compared to the one or one and a half per cent found in Canadian or United

States ores. There was tin, zinc, cobalt, cadmium, tungsten, diamonds — Nature had put a (veritable) treasure chest right under the pirates' noses, and here was this disagreeable humorist who refused to stick to his puns, and this Congo Reform Association and assorted do-gooders and moralists disturbing what promised to be one of the world's biggest bonanzas! Something had to be done.

Something was done. In 1908, the Congo Free State was taken out of the King's hands and simply annexed to Belgium. The profits, instead of being sifted through Leopold's fingers, flowed directly into the vaults of the corporations, Belgian, British, and American. Under the benevolent rule of the Belgian parliament, the cutting off of human hands was discontinued, but not so the practice of forced labor. In 1948, three years after Hitler's suicide in a dug-out deep under Berlin's Wilhelmstrasse, two Czech travelers report that native road gangs in the Congo kneel in the dust until the whites in their car pass out of sight. Under the benevolent rule of the Belgian parliament, Congolese natives are excluded from high school or university education; so that on the day of Congo independence, July 1, 1960, we find among a population of fourteen million souls exactly sixteen (16) Congolese graduates of universities or higher technical schools; of these sixteen, only three (3) had studied in Belgium. At the University of Leopoldville — there actually is such a thing! — were 2,000 places in 1959, with a total of twelve (12) Congolese graduates. Under the benevolent rule of the Belgian parliament, Leopold's marauding, mutilating, massacring soldiery was continued in full flower, 2,000 men, officered by 1,000 whites. Under the benevolent rule of the Belgian parliament, everything was done to keep the native population in illiterate darkness, superstition, internecine hatred — five hundred tribes speaking two hundred differing idioms, some living under conditions of primitive communism, some having reached the first stages of slave economy, some utilized as serfs and servants of the conquering whites, and some, mainly the Katanga miners, propelled in one giant push from tribal society into modern capitalist exploitation.

On top of that — uranium. In 1922, uranium was discovered at Shinkolobve, near Jadotville, and today, the Congo is the capitalist world's biggest uranium producer. As a by-product, they get germanium — "one ton a year, here," stated Mr. Rijckman of the Union Minière Prince Leopold Mine in 1948, and added, "we could produce up to one hundred tons, but we don't want to depress world market prices."

Uranium furnishes atomic energy; germanium is the base of modern electronics — and all of this in one province of the Congo! What a plum!

What a plum! What glorious prospects, considering that the Union Minière's lease in Katanga runs until March 11, 1990! No wonder they killed a man like Lumumba and hate all those Congolese — "monkeys," they call them — who want independence for themselves, and a unified Congo State to take its place in dignity and freedom at the side of all the other newly liberated nations of Africa and Asia, at the side of all the free peoples of the world. No wonder King Leopold's legitimate and not so legitimate heirs rejoice in the plans and actions of characters like Mobuto and Tshombe, who are today's version of the fratricidal cannibal chief Mulunba N'Cusa, the inventor of the "death trap" described by Mark Twain.

And just as Mark Twain's day saw international conferences used to cover up international crime, so today. Just as Mark Twain's day saw newspapermen and professors, politicians and cardinals banded to hoodwink the public, so today.

But there is one difference — *the* difference, you might say. Mark Twain conducted his fight in a period when the great monopolistic empires were still in the ascendancy, when socialism was an untried theory, when freedom and independence for people of colored skin were only a dream suffocated in blood. Today, one third of the globe marches under the banner of socialism; another third has shaken off its colonial chains; and the current King Leopolds hide behind the flag of the United Nations.

Mark Twain, were he with us, would feel most encouraged. He would continue to call a sham, a sham, and a brute, a brute. But he would also see confirmed his own prophecy of the new world coming, the world of the laboring man — "It is not long to wait; his day is close at hand: his clans are gathering, they are on their way; his bugles are sounding the call, they are answering; every week that comes and goes, sees ten thousand new crusaders swing into line and add their pulsing footfalls to the thunder-tread of his mighty battalions."

STEFAN HEYM

27

MARK TWAIN
KING LEOPOLD'S SOLILOQUY

"It Is I"

Leopold II is the absolute Master of the whole of the internal and external activity of the Independent State of the Congo. The organization of justice, the army, the industrial and commercial regimes are established freely by himself. He would say, and with greater accuracy than did Louis XIV, "The State, it is I." *Prof. F. Cattier, Brussels University.*

Let us repeat after so many others what has become a platitude, the success of the African work is the work of a sole directing will, without being hampered by the hesitation of timorous politicians, carried out under his sole responsibility — intelligent, thoughtful, conscious of the perils and the advantages, discounting with an admirable prescience the great results of a near future. *M. Alfred Poskine in "Bilans Congolais."*

KING LEOPOLD'S SOLILOQUY

[*Throws down pamphlets which he has been reading. Excitedly combs his flowing spread of whiskers with big fingers; pounds the table with big fists; lets off brisk volleys of unsanctified language at brief intervals, repentantly drooping his head, between volleys, and kissing the Louis XI crucifix hanging from his neck, accompanying the kisses with mumbled apologies; presently rises, flushed and perspiring, and walks the floor, gesticulating*]

— — !! — — !! If I had them by the throat! [*Hastily kisses the crucifix, and mumbles*] In these twenty years I have spent millions to keep the press of the two hemispheres quiet, and still these leaks keep on occurring. I have spent other millions on religion and art, and what do I get for it? Nothing. Not a compliment. These generosities are studiedly ignored, in print. In print I get nothing but slanders — and slanders again — and still slanders, and slanders on top of slanders! Grant them true, what of it? They are slanders all the same, when uttered against a king.

Miscreants — they are telling *everything!* Oh, everything: how I went pilgriming among the Powers in tears, with my mouth full of Bible and my pelt oozing piety at every pore, and implored them to place the vast and rich and populous Congo Free State in trust in my hands as their agent, so that I might root out slavery and stop the slave raids, and lift up those twenty-five millions of gentle and harmless blacks out of darkness into light, the light of our blessed Redeemer, the light that streams from his holy Word, the light that makes glorious our noble civilization—lift them up and dry their tears and fill their bruised hearts with joy and gratitude — lift them up and make them comprehend that they were no longer outcasts and forsaken, but our very brothers in Christ; how

America and thirteen great European states wept in sympathy with me, and were persuaded; how their representatives met in convention in Berlin and made me Head Foreman and Superintendent of the Congo State, and drafted out my powers and limitations, carefully guarding the persons and liberties and properties of the natives against hurt and harm; forbidding whisky traffic and gun traffic; providing courts of justice; making commerce free and fetterless to the merchants and traders of all nations, and welcoming and safeguarding all missionaries of all creeds and denominations. They have told how I planned and prepared my establishment and selected my horde of officials — "pals" and "pimps" of mine, "unspeakable Belgians" every one — and hoisted my flag, and "took in" a President of the United States, and got him to be the first to recognize it and salute it. Oh, well, let them blackguard me if they like; it is a deep satisfaction to me to remember that I was a shade too smart for that nation that thinks itself so smart. Yes, I certainly did bunco a Yankee — as those people phrase it. Pirate flag? Let them call it so — perhaps it is. All the same, *they were the first to salute it.*

*They were the
first to salute it!*

These meddlesome American missionaries!
these frank British consuls! these blabbing
Belgian-born traitor officials! — those tire-
some parrots are always talking, always telling. They have told how for twenty years I
have ruled the Congo State not as a trustee
of the Powers, an agent, a subordinate, a
foreman, but as a sovereign — sovereign over
a fruitful domain four times as large as the
German Empire — sovereign absolute, irre-
sponsible, above all law; trampling the Berlin-
made Congo charter under foot; barring out

all foreign traders but myself; restricting commerce to myself, through concessionaires who are my creatures and confederates; seizing and holding the State as my personal property, the whole of its vast revenues as my private "swag" — mine, solely mine — claiming and holding its millions of people as my private property, my serfs, my slaves; their labor mine, with or without wage; the food they raise not their property but mine; the rubber, the ivory and all the other riches of the land mine — mine solely — and gathered for me by the men, the women and the little children under compulsion of lash and bullet, fire, starvation, mutilation-and the halter.

These pests! — it is as I say, they have kept back nothing! They have revealed these and yet other details which shame should have kept them silent about, since they were exposures of a king, a sacred personage and immune from reproach, by right of his selection and appointment to his great office by God himself; a king whose acts cannot be criticized without blasphemy, since God has observed them from the beginning and has manifested no dissatisfaction with them, nor shown disapproval of them, nor hampered nor interrupted them in any way. By this sign I recognize his approval of what I have done;

his cordial and glad approval, I am sure I may say.

Blest, crowned, beatified with this great reward, this golden reward, this unspeakably precious reward, why should I care for men's cursings and revilings of me? *[With a sudden outburst of feeling]* May they roast a million aeons in —

[Catches his breath and effusively kisses the crucifix; sorrowfully murmurs, "I shall get myself damned yet, with these indiscretions of speech."]

Yes, they go on telling everything, these chatterers! They tell how I levy incredibly burdensome taxes upon the natives — taxes which are a pure theft; taxes which they must satisfy by gathering rubber under hard and constantly harder conditions, and by raising and furnishing food supplies gratis — and it all comes out that, when they fall short of their tasks through hunger, sickness, despair, and ceaseless and exhausting labor without rest, and forsake their homes and flee to the woods to escape punishment, my black soldiers, drawn from unfriendly tribes, and instigated and directed by my Belgians, hunt them down and butcher them and burn their villages — reserving some of the girls. They tell it all: how I am wiping a nation of friend-less creatures out of existence by every form of murder, for my private pocket's sake, and how every shilling I get costs a rape, a mutilation or a life. But they never say, although they know it, that I have labored in the cause of religion at the same time and all the time, and have sent missionaries there (of a "convenient stripe," as they phrase it), to teach them the error of their ways and bring them to Him who is all mercy and love, and who is the sleepless guardian and friend of all who suffer. They tell only what is against me, they will not tell what is in my favor.

They tell how England required of me a Commission of Inquiry into Congo atrocities, and how, to quiet that meddling country, with its disagreeable Congo Reform Association, made up of earls and bishops and John Morleys and university grandees and other dudes, more interested in other people's business than in their own, I appointed it. Did it stop their mouths? No, they merely pointed out that it was a commission composed wholly of my "Congo butchers," "the very men whose acts were to be inquired into." They said it was equivalent to appointing a commission of wolves to inquire into depredations committed upon a sheepfold. *Nothing* can satisfy a cursed Englishman!*

And were the fault-finders frank with my private character? They could not be more so if I were a plebeian, a peasant, a medianic. They remind the world that from the earliest days my house has been chapel and brothel combined, and both industries working full time; that I practiced cruelties upon my queen and my daughters, and supplemented them with daily shame and humiliations; that, when my queen lay in the happy refuge of her coffin, and a daughter implored me on her knees to let her look for the last time upon her mother's face, I refused; and that, three years ago, not being satisfied with the stolen spoils of a whole alien nation, I robbed my own child of her property and appeared

* This visit had a more fortunate result than was anticipated. One member of the Commission was a leading Congo official, another an official of the government in Belgium, the third a Swiss jurist. It was feared that the work of the Commission would not be more genuine than that of innumerable so-called "investigations" by local officials. But it appears that the Commission was met by a very avalanche of awful testimony. One who was present at a public hearing writes: "Men of stone would be moved by the stories that are being unfolded as the Commission probes into the awful history of rubber collection." it is evident the commissioners were moved. Of their report and its bearing upon the international issue presented by the conceded conditions in the Congo State, something is said on a supplementary page of this pamphlet. Certain reforms were ordered by the Commission of Inquiry in the one section visited, but the latest word is that after its departure conditions were soon worse than before its coming. — M. T.

38

by proxy in court, a spectacle to the civilized world, to defend the act and complete the crime. It is as I have said: they are unfair, unjust; they will resurrect and give new currency to such things as those, or to any other things that count against me, but they will not mention any act of mine that is in my favor. I have spent more money on art than any other monarch of my time, and they know it. Do they speak of it, do they tell about it? No, they do not. They prefer to work up what they call "ghastly statistics" into offensive kindergarten object lessons, whose purpose is to make sentimental people shudder, and prejudice them against me. They remark that "if the innocent blood shed in the Congo State by King Leopold were put in buckets and the buckets placed side by side, the line would stretch 2,000 miles; if the skeletons of his ten millions of starved and butchered dead could rise up and march in single file, it would take them seven months and four days to pass a given point; if compacted together in a body, they would occupy more ground than St. Louis covers, World's Fair and all; if they should all clap their bony hands at once, the grisly crash would be heard at a distance of —" Damnation, it makes me tired! And they do similar miracles with the money I have distilled from that blood and put into my pocket. They pile it into Egyptian pyramids; they carpet Saharas with it; they spread it across the sky, and the shadow it casts makes twilight in the earth. And the tears I have caused, the hearts I have broken — oh, nothing can persuade them to let *them* alone!

[Meditative pause] Well ... no matter, I *did* beat the Yankees, anyway! there's comfort in that.

[Reads with mocking smile, the President's Order of Recognition of April 22, 1884]

. . . the government of the United States announces its sympathy with and approval of the humane and benevolent purposes of (my Congo scheme), and will order the officers of the United States, both on land and sea, to recognize its flag as the flag of a friendly government.

Possibly the Yankees would like to take that back, now, but they will find that my agents are not over there in America for nothing. But there is no danger; neither nations nor governments can afford to confess a blunder.

[*With a contented smile, begins to read from "Report by Rev. W. M. Morrison, American missionary in the Congo Free State"*]

*

I furnish herewith some of the many atrocious incidents which have come under my own personal observation; they reveal the *organized* system of plunder and outrage which has been perpetrated and is now being carried on in that unfortunate country by King Leopold of Belgium. I say King Leopold, because he and he *alone* is now responsible, since he is the *absolute sovereign. He styles himself such.* When our government in 1884 laid the foundation of the Congo Free State, by recognizing its flag, little did it know that this concern, parading under the guise of philanthropy — was really King Leopold of Belgium, one of the shrewdest, most heartless and most conscienceless rulers that ever sat on a throne. This is apart from his known corrupt morals, which have made his name and his family a byword in two continents. Our government would most certainly not have recognized that flag had it known that it was really King Leopold individually who was asking for recognition; had it known that it was setting up in the heart of Africa an *absolute monarchy;* had it known that, having put down African slavery in our own country at great cost of blood and money, it was *establishing a worse form of slavery right in Africa.*

[*With evil joy*] Yes, I certainly was a shade too clever for the Yankees. It hurts; it gravels

41

them. They can't get over it! Puts a shame upon them in another way, too, and a graver way; for they never can rid their records of the reproachful fact that their vain Republic, self-appointed Champion and Promoter of the Liberties of the World, is the only democracy in history that has lent its power and influence to the establishing of an *absolute monarchy!*

[*Contemplating, with an unfriendly eye, a stately pile of pamphlets*] Blister the meddlesome missionaries! They write tons of these things. They seem to be always around, always spying, always eye-witnessing the happenings; and everything they see they commit to paper. They are always prowling from place to place; the natives consider them their only friends; they go to them with their sorrows; they show them their scars and their wounds,

The natives go to them with their sorrows.

inflicted by my soldier police; they hold up the stumps of their arms and lament because their hands have been chopped off, as punishment for not bringing in enough rubber, and as proof to be laid before my officers that the required punishment was well and truly carried out. One of these missionaries saw eighty-one of these hands drying over a fire for transmission to my officials — and of course he must go and set it down and print it. They travel and travel, they spy and spy! And nothing is too trivial for them to print.

[*Takes up a pamphlet. Reads a passage from Report of a "Journey made in July, August and September, 1903, by Rev. A. E. Scrivener, a British missionary"*]

.... Soon we began talking, and without any encouragement on my part the natives began the tales I had become so accustomed to. They were living in peace and quietness when the white men came in from the lake with all sorts of requests to do this and that, and they thought it meant slavery. So they attempted to keep the white men out of their country but without avail. The rifles were too much for them. So they submitted and made up their minds to do the best they could under the altered circumstances. First came the command to build houses for the soldiers, and this was done without a murmur. Then they had to feed the soldiers and all the men and women — hangers on — who accompanied them. Then they were told to bring in rubber. This was quite a new thing for them to do. There was rubber in the forest several days away from their home, but that it was worth anything was news to them. A small reward was offered and a rush was made for the rubber. "What strange white men, to give us cloth and beads for the sap of a wild vine." They rejoiced in what they thought their good fortune. But soon the reward was reduced until at last they were told to bring in the rubber for nothing. To this they tried to demur; but to their great surprise several were shot by the soldiers, and the rest were told, with many curses and blows, to go at once or more would be killed. Terrified, they began to prepare their food for the fortnight's absence from the village which the collection of rubber entailed. The soldiers discovered them sitting about. "What, not gone yet?" Bang! bang! bang! and down fell one and another, dead, in the midst of wives and companions. There is a terrible wail and an attempt made to prepare the dead for burial, but this is not allowed. All must go at once to the forest. Without food? Yes, without food. And off the poor wretches had to go without even their tinder boxes to make fires. Many died in the forests of hunger and exposure, and still more from the rifles of the ferocious soldiers in charge of the post. In spite of all their efforts the amount fell off and more and more were killed. I was shown around the place, and the sites of former big chiefs' settlements were pointed out. A careful estimate made the population of, say, seven years ago, to be 2, 000 people in and about the post, within a radius of, say, a quarter of a mile. All told, they would not

*Some bones which
they had seen ...*

muster 200 now, and there is so much sadness and
gloom about them that they are fast decreasing.

We stayed there all day on Monday and had many
talks with the people. On the Sunday some of the
boys had told me of some bones which they had
seen, so on the Monday I asked to be shown these
bones. Lying about on the grass, within a few yards
of the house I was occupying, were numbers of
human skulls, bones, in some cases complete skeletons. I counted thirty-six skulls, and saw many sets of
bones from which the skulls were missing. I called
one of the men and asked the meaning of it. "When
the rubber palaver began," said he, "the soldiers shot
so many we grew tired of burying, and very often we
were not allowed to bury; and so just dragged the

bodies out into the grass and left them. There are
hundred all around if you would like to see them."
But I had seen more than enough, and was sickened
by the stories that came from men and women alike
of the awful time they had passed through. The
Bulgarian atrocities might be considered as mildness
itself when compared with what was done here. How
the people submitted I don't know, and even now I
wonder as I think of their patience. That some of
them managed to run away is some cause for thank-
fulness. I stayed there two days and the one thing
that impressed itself upon me was the collection of
rubber. I saw long files of men come in, as at Bongo,
with their little baskets under their arms; saw them
paid their milk tin full of salt, and the two yards of
calico flung to the headmen; saw their trembling
timidity, and in fact a great deal that all went to
prove the state of terrorism that exists and the vir-
tual slavery in which the people are held.

That is their way; they spy and spy, and run
into print with every foolish trifle. And that
British consul, Mr. Casement, is just like
them. He gets hold of a *diary which had been
kept by one of my government officers,* and, although it is a private diary and intended for
no eye but its owner's, Mr. Casement is so
lacking in delicacy and refinement as to print
passages from it.

[*Reads a passage from the diary*]

Each time the corporal goes out to get rubber, cartridges are given him. He must bring back all not used, and for every one used he must bring back a right hand. M. P. told me that sometimes they shot a cartridge at an animal in hunting; they then cut off a hand from a living man. As to the extent to which this is carried on, he informed me that in six months the State on the Mambogo River had used 6,000 cartridges, which means that 6,000 people are killed or mutilated. It means more than 6,000 ... for the people have told me repeatedly that the soldiers kill the children with the butt of their guns.

When the subtle consul thinks silence will be more effective than words, he employs it. Here he leaves it to be recognized that a thousand killings and mutilations a month is a large output for so small a region as the Mambogo River concession, silently indicating the dimensions of it by accompanying his report with a map of the prodigious Congo State, in which there is not room for so small an object as that river. That silence is intended to say, "If it is a thousand a month in this little corner, imagine the output of the whole vast State!" A gentleman would not descend to these furtivenesses.

Now as to the mutilations. You can't head off a Congo critic and make him stay headed-off; he dodges, and straightway comes back at you from another direction. They are full of slippery arts. When the mutilations (severing hands, unsexing men, etc.) began to stir Europe, we hit upon the idea of excusing them with a retort which we judged would knock them dizzy on that subject for good and all, and leave them nothing more to say; to wit, we boldly laid the custom on the natives, and said we did not invent it, but only followed it. Did it knock them dizzy? did it shut their mouths? Not for an hour. They dodged, and came straight back at us with the remark that "if a Christian king can perceive a saving moral difference between inventing bloody barbarities, and *imitating them from savages,* for charity's sake let him get what comfort he can out of his confession!"

It is most amazing, the way that that consul acts — that spy, that busy-body.

[*Takes up pamphlet "Treatment of Women and Children in the Congo State; what Mr. Casement Saw in 1903"*]

Hardly two years ago! Intruding that date upon the public was a piece of cold malice. It is intended to weaken the force of my press syndicate's assurances to the public that my severities in the Congo *ceased,* and ceased utterly, *years and years ago.* This man is fond of trifles — revels in them, gloats over them, pets them, fondles them, sets them all down. One doesn't need to drowse through his monotonous report to see that; the mere subheadings of its chapters prove it. [*Reads*]

> Two hundred and forty persons, *men, women and children*, compelled to supply government with *one ton* of carefully prepared foodstuffs *per week*, receiving in remuneration all told, the princely sum of 15s 10d.!

Very well, it was liberal. It was not much short of a penny a week for each nigger. It suits this consul to belittle it, yet he knows very well that I could have had both the food and the labor for nothing. I can prove it by a thousand instances. [*Reads*]

> Expedition against a village behindhand in its (compulsory) supplies; result, slaughter of sixteen persons; among them three women and a boy of five years. Ten carried off, to be prisoners till ransomed; among them a child, who died during the march.

But he is careful not to explain that we are *obliged* to resort to ransom to collect debts, where the people have nothing to pay with. Families that escape to the woods sell some of their members into slavery and thus provide the ransom. He knows that I would stop this if I could find a less objectionable way to collect their debts. . . . Mm — here is some more of the consul's delicacy! He reports a conversation he had with some natives:

> Q. How do you know it was the *white* men themselves who ordered these cruel things to be done to you? These things must have been done without the white man's knowledge by the black soldiers.
>
> A.These white men told their soldiers: "You only kill *women;* you cannot kill men. You must prove that you kill men." So then the soldiers when they killed us (here he stopped and hesitated and then pointing to ... he said:) then they ... and took them to the white men, who said: "It is true, you have killed *men.*"
>
> Q.You say this is true? Were many of you so treated after being shot?
>
> All [*shouting out*]: Nkoto! Nkoto! (Very many! Very many!)
>
> There was no doubt that these people were not inventing. Their vehemence, their flashing eyes, their excitement, were not simulated.

Of course the critic had to divulge that; he has no self-respect. All his kind reproach me, although they know quite well that I took no pleasure in punishing the men in that particular way, but only did it as a warning to other delinquents. Ordinary punishments are no good, with ignorant savages; they make no impression.

[Reads more sub-heads]

Devastated region; population reduced from 40,000 to 8,000.

He does not take the trouble to say how it happened. He is fertile in concealments. He hopes his readers and his Congo reformers, of the Lord-Aberdeen-Norbury-John-Morley-Sir-Gilbert-Parker stripe, will think they were all killed. They were not. The great majority of them escaped. They fled to the bush with their families because of the rubber raids, and it was there they died of hunger. Could we help that?

One of my sorrowing critics observes: "Other Christian rulers tax their people, but

furnish schools, courts of law, roads, light, water and protection to life and limb in return; King Leopold taxes his stolen nation, but provides *nothing in return but hunger, terror, grief, shame, captivity, mutilation and massacre.*" That is their style! I furnish "nothing"! I send the gospel to the survivors; these censure-mongers know it, but they would rather have their tongues cut out than mention it. I have several times required my raiders to give the dying an opportunity to kiss the sacred emblem; and if they obeyed me I have without doubt been the humble means of saving many souls. None of my (traducers) have had the fairness to mention this; but let it pass; there is One who has not overlooked it, and that is my solace, that is my consolation.

[*Puts down the Report, takes up a pamphlet, glances along the middle of it.*]

This is where the "death-trap" comes in. Meddlesome missionary spying around — Rev. W. H. Sheppard. Talks with a black raider of mine after a raid; cozens him into giving away some particulars. The raider remarks:

"I demanded 30 slaves from this side of the stream and 30 from the other side; 2 points of ivory, 2,500 balls of rubber, 13 goats, 10 fowls and 6 dogs, some corn chumy, etc."

"How did the fight come up?" I asked.

"I sent for all their chiefs, sub-chiefs, men and women, to come on a certain day, saying that I was going to finish all the (palaver) When they entered these small gates (the walls being made of fences brought from other villages, the high native ones) I demanded all my pay or I would kill them; so they refused to pay me, and I ordered the fence to be closed so they couldn't run away; then we killed them here inside the fence. The panels of the fence fell down and some escaped."

"How many did you kill?" I asked.

"We killed plenty, will you see some of them?"

That was just what I wanted.

He said: "I think we have killed between eighty and ninety, and those in the other villages I don't know, I did not go out but sent my people."

He and I walked out on the plain just near the camp. There were three dead bodies with the flesh carved off from the waist down.

"Why are they carved so, only leaving the bones?" I asked.

"My people ate them," he answered promptly. He then explained, "The men who have young children do not eat people, but all the rest ate them."

On the left was a big man, shot in the back and without a head. (All corpses were nude.)

"Where is the man's head?" I asked.

"Oh, they made a bowl of the forehead to rub up tobacco and (diamba) in."

We continued to walk and examine until late in the afternoon, and counted forty-one bodies. The rest had been eaten up by the people.

On returning to the camp, we crossed a young woman, shot in the back of the head, one hand was cut away. I asked why, and Mulunba N'Cusa explained that they always cut off the right hand to give to the State on their return.

"Can you not show me some of the hands?" I asked.

So he conducted us to a framework of sticks, under which was burning a slow fire, and there they were, the right hands — I counted eighty-one in all.

There were not less than sixty women (Bena Pianga) prisoners, I saw them.

We say that we have as fully as possible investigated the whole outrage, and find it was a plan previously made to get all the stuff possible and to catch and kill the poor people in the death-trap.

Another detail, as we see! — cannibalism. They report cases of it with a most offensive frequency. My traducers do not forget to remark that, inasmuch as I am absolute and with a word can prevent in the Congo anything I choose to prevent, then whatsoever is done there by my permission is my act, my *personal* act; that I do it; that the hand of my agent is as truly *my* hand as if it were attached to my own arm; and so they picture me in my robes of state, with my crown on my head, munching human flesh, saying grace, mumbling thanks to Him from whom all good things come. Dear, dear, when the soft-hearts get hold of a thing like that missionary's contribution they completely lose their tranquillity over it. They speak profanely and reproach Heaven for allowing such a fiend to live. Meaning me. They think it irregular. They go shuddering around, brooding over the reduction of that Congo population from 25,000,000 to 15,000,000 in the twenty years of my administration; then they burst out and call me "the King with Ten Million Murders on his Soul." They call me a "record." The most of them do not stop with charging merely the 10,000,000 against me. No, they reflect that but for me the population, by natural increase, would now be 30,000,000, so they charge another 5,000,000 against me and make my total death-harvest 15,000,000. They remark that the man who killed the goose that laid the golden egg was responsible for the eggs she would subsequently have laid if she had been let alone. Oh, yes, they call me a "record." They remark that twice in a generation, in India, the Great Famine destroys 2,000,000 out of a population of

320,000,000, and the whole world holds up its hands in pity and horror; then they fall to wondering where the world would find room for its emotions if I had a chance to trade places with the Great Famine for twenty years! The idea fires their fancy, and they go on and imagine the Famine coming in state at the end of the twenty years and prostrating itself before me, saying: "Teach me, Lord, I perceive that I am but an apprentice." And next they imagine Death coming, with his scythe and hour-glass, and begging me to marry his daughter and reorganize his plant and run the business. For the whole world, you see! By this time their diseased minds are under full steam, and they get down their books and expand their labors, with me for text. They hunt through all biography for my match, working Attila, Torquemada, Ghengis Khan, Ivan the Terrible, and the rest of that crowd for all they are worth, and evilly exulting when they cannot find it. Then they examine the historical earthquakes and cyclones and blizzards and cataclysms and volcanic eruptions: verdict, none of them "in it" with me. At last they do really hit it (as they think), and they close their labors with conceding — reluctantly — that I have one match in history, but only one — the *Flood*. This is intemperate.

But they are always that, when they think of me. They can no more keep quiet when my name is mentioned than can a glass of water control its feelings with a seidlitz powder in its bowels. The bizarre things they can imagine, with me for an inspiration! One Englishman offers to give me the odds of three to one and bet me anything I like, up to 20,000 guineas, that for 2,000,000 years I am going to be the most conspicuous foreigner in hell. The man is so beside himself with anger that he does not perceive that the idea is foolish. Foolish and unbusinesslike: you see, there could be no winner; both of us would be losers, on account of the loss of interest on the stakes; at four or five per cent compounded, this would amount to — I do not know how much, exactly, but, by the time the term was up and the bet payable, a person could buy hell itself with the accumulation.

Another madman wants to construct a memorial for the perpetuation of my name, out of my 15,000,000 skulls and skeletons, and is full of vindictive enthusiasm over his strange project. He has it all ciphered out and drawn to scale. Out of the skulls he will build a combined monument and mausoleum to me which shall exactly duplicate the Great Pyramid of Cheops, whose base covers thirteen acres, and whose apex is 451 feet above ground. He desires to stuff me and stand me up in the sky on that apex, robed and crowned, with my "pirate flag" in one hand and a butcher-knife and pendant handcuffs in the other. He will build the pyramid in the center of a depopulated tract, a brooding solitude covered with weeds and the mouldering ruins of burned villages, where the spirits of the starved and murdered dead will voice their laments forever in the whispers of the wandering winds. Radiating from the pyramid, like the spokes of a wheel, there are to be forty grand avenues of approach, each thirty-five miles long, and each fenced on both sides by skulless skeletons standing a yard and a half apart and festooned together in line by short chains stretching from wrist to wrist and attached to tried and true old handcuffs stamped with my private trademark, a crucifix and butcher-knife crossed, with motto, "By this sign we prosper"; each osseous fence to consist of 2,00,000 skeletons on a side, which is 400,000 to each avenue. It is remarked with satisfaction that it aggregates three or four thousand miles (single-ranked) of skeletons — 15,000,000 all told — and would stretch across America from New York to San Francisco. It is remarked further, in the hopeful tone of a railroad company forecasting showy extensions of its mileage, that my output is 500,000 corpses a year when my plant is running full time, and that therefore if I am spared ten years longer there will be fresh skulls enough to add 175 feet to the pyramid, making it by a long way the loftiest architectural construction on the earth, and fresh skeletons enough to continue the transcontinental file (on piles) a thousand miles into the Pacific. The cost of gathering the materials from my "widely scattered and innumerable private graveyards," and transporting them, and building the monument and the radiating grand avenues, is duly ciphered out, running into an aggregate of millions of guineas, and then — why then, (— — !! — — !!) this idiot asks me *to furnish the money!* [*Sudden and effusive application of the crucifix*] He reminds me that my yearly income from the Congo is millions of guineas, and that only 5,000,000 would be required for his enterprise. Every day wild attempts are made upon my purse; they do not affect me, they cost me not a thought. But *this one* — this one troubles me, makes me

*Women chained by the neck
by rubber sentries.*

nervous; for there is no telling what an un-
hinged creature like this may think of next....
If he should think of Carnegie — but I must ban-
ish that thought out of my mind! it worries
my days; it troubles my sleep. That way lies
madness. [*After a pause*] There is no other
way — I have got to buy Carnegie.

[*Harassed and muttering, walks the floor a
while, then takes to the Consul's chapter-headings
again. Reads*]

Government starved a woman's children to death
and killed her sons.

Butchery of women and children.

The native has been converted into a being without ambition because without hope.

Women chained by the neck by rubber sentries.

Women refuse to bear children because, with a baby to carry, they cannot well run away and hide from the soldiers.

Statement of a child: "I, my mother, my grandmother and my sister, we ran away into the bush. A great number of our people were killed by the soldiers. . . . After that they saw a little bit of my mother's head, and the soldiers ran quickly to where we were and caught my grandmother, my mother, my sister and another little one younger than us. Each wanted my mother for a wife, and argued about it, so they finally decided to kill her. They shot her through the stomach with a gun and she fell, and when I saw that I cried very much, because they killed my grandmother and mother and I was left alone. I saw it all done!"

It has a sort of pitiful sound, although they are only blacks. It carries me back and back into the past, to when my children were little, and would fly — to the bush, so to speak — when they saw me coming....

[Resumes the reading of chapter-headings of the Consul's report]

They put a knife through a child's stomach.

They cut off the hands and brought them to C. D. (white officer) and spread them out in a row for him to see. They left them lying there, because the white man had seen them, so they did not need to take them to P.

Captured children left in the bush to die, by the soldiers.

Friends came to ransom a captured girl; but sentry refused, saying the white man wanted her because she was young.

Extract from a native girl's testimony:

"On our way the soldiers saw a little child, and when they went to kill it the child laughed, so the soldier took the butt of his gun and struck the child with it and then cut off its head. One day they killed my half-sister and cut off her head, hands and feet, because she had bangles on. Then they caught another sister, and sold her to the W. W. people and now she is a slave there."

The little child laughed! [*A long pause. Musing*] That innocent creature. Somehow — I wish it had not laughed.

[*Reads*]

Mutilated children.

Government encouragement of inter-tribal slave. traffic. The monstrous fines levied upon villages tardy in their supplies of foodstuffs compel the natives to sell their fellows — and children — to other tribes in order to meet the fine.

A father and mother forced to sell their boy.

Widow forced to sell her little girl.

[*Irritated*] Hang the monotonous grumbler, what would he have me do! Let a widow off merely because she is a widow? He knows quite well that there is nothing much left, now, *but* widows. I have nothing against widows, as a class, but business is business, and I've got to live, haven't I, even if it does cause inconvenience to somebody here and there?

[*Reads*]

Men intimidated by the torture of their wives and daughters. (To make the men furnish rubber and supplies and so get their captured women released from chains and detention.) The sentry explained to me that he caught the women and brought them in (chained together neck to neck) by direction of his employer.

An agent explained that he was forced to catch women in preference to men, as then the men brought in supplies quicker; but he did not explain how the children deprived of their parents obtained their own food supplies.

A file of 15 (captured) women.

Allowing women and children to die of starvation in prison.

[*Musing*] Death from *hunger*. A lingering, long misery that must be. Days and days, and still days and days, the forces of the body failing, dribbling away, little by little — yes, it must be the hardest death of all. And to see food carried by, every day, and you can have none of it! Of course the little children cry for it, and that wrings the mother's heart....

[*A sigh*] Ah, well, it cannot be helped; circumstances make this discipline necessary.

[Reads]

The crucifying of sixty women!

How stupid, how tactless! Christendom's goose flesh will rise with horror at the news. "Profanation of the sacred emblem!" That is what Christendom will shout. Yes, Christendom will buzz. It can hear me charged with half a million murders a year for twenty years and keep its composure, but to profane the Symbol is quite another matter. It will regard this as serious. It will wake up and want to look into my record. Buzz? Indeed it will; I seem to hear the distant hum already.... It was wrong to crucify the women, clearly wrong, manifestly wrong, I can see it now, myself, and am sorry it happened, sincerely sorry. I believe it would have answered just as well to skin them.... [*With a sigh*] But none of us thought of that; one cannot think of everything; and after all it is but human to err.

It will make a stir, no doubt, these crucifixions. Persons will begin to ask once more, as now and then in times past, how I can hope to win and keep the respect of the human race if I continue to give up my life to murder and pillage. [*Scornfully*] When have they heard me say I wanted the respect of the human race? Do they confuse me with the common herd? Do they forget that I am a king? What king has valued the respect of the human race? I mean deep down in his private heart. If they would reflect, they would know that it is impossible that a king should value the respect of the human race. He stands upon an eminence and looks out over the world and sees multitudes of meek human things worshiping the persons, and submitting to the oppressions and exactions, of a dozen human things who are in no way better or finer than themselves — made on just their own pattern, in fact, and out of the same quality of mud. When it *talks*, it is a race of whales; but a king knows it for a race of tadpoles. Its history gives it away. If men

Made on just their own pattern.

were really *men*, how could a Czar be possible? And how could I be possible? But we *are* possible; we are quite safe; and with God's help we shall continue the business at the old stand. It will be found that the race will put up with us, in its docile immemorial way. It may pull a wry face now and then, and make large talk, but it will stay on its knees all the same.

Making large talk is one of its specialties. It works itself up, and froths at the mouth, and just when you think it is going to throw a brick — it heaves a poem! Lord, what a race it is!

A CZAR — 1905

A pasteboard autocrat; a despot out of date;
A fading planet in the glare of day;
A flickering candle in the bright sun's ray,
Burnt to the socket; fruit left too late,
High on a blighted bough, ripe till it's rotten.

By God forsaken and by time forgotten,
Watching the crumbling edges of his lands,
A spineless god to whom dumb millions pray,
From Finland in the West to far Cathay,
Lord of a frost-bound continent he stands,
Her seeming ruin his dim mind appalls,

And in the frozen stupor of his sleep
He hears dull thunders, pealing as she falls,
And mighty fragments dropping in the deep.*

It is fine, one is obliged to concede it; it is a great picture, and impressive. The mongrel handles his pen well. Still, with opportunity, I would cruci... flay him. "A spineless god." It is the Czar to a dot — a god, and spineless; a royal invertebrate, poor lad; soft-hearted and out of place. "A spineless god *to whom dumb millions pray.*"

Remorselessly correct; concise, too, compact — the soul and spirit of the human race compressed into half a sentence. On their knees — 140,000,000. On their knees to a little tin deity. Massed together, they would stretch away, and away, and away, across the plains, fading and dimming and failing in a measureless perspective — why, even the telescope's vision could not reach to the final frontier of that continental spread of human servility. Now *why* should a king value the respect of the human race? It is quite unreasonable to expect it. A curious race, certainly! It finds fault with me and with my occupations, and forgets that neither of us could

* B. H. Nadal, in *New York Times.*

exist an hour without its sanction. It is our confederate and all-powerful protector. It is our bulwark, our friend, our fortress. For this it has our gratitude, our deep and honest gratitude — but not our respect. Let it snivel and fret and grumble if it likes; that is all right; we do not mind that.

[Turns over leaves of a scrapbook, pausing now and then to read a clipping and make a comment]

The poets — how they do hunt that poor Czar! French, Germans, English, Americans — they all have a bark at him. The finest and capablest of the pack, and the fiercest, are Swinburne (English, I think), and a pair of Americans, Thomas Bailey Aldrich and Colonel Richard Waterson Gilder, of the sentimental periodical called *Century Magazine* and *Louisville Courier-Journal.* They certainly have uttered some very strong yelps. I can't seem to find them — I must have mislaid them.... If a poet's bite were as terrible as his bark, why dear me — but it isn't. A wise king minds neither of them; but the poet doesn't know it. It's a case of little dog and lightning express. When the Czar goes thundering by, the poet skips out and rages alongside for a little distance, then returns to his kennel wagging his head with satisfaction, and thinks he has inflicted a memorable scare, whereas nothing has really happened — the Czar didn't know he was around. They never bark at me; I wonder why that is. I suppose my Corruption Department buys them. That must be it, for certainly I ought to inspire a bark or two; I'm rather choice material, I should say. Why — here *is* a yelp at me.

[*Mumbling a poem*]

> ... What gives thee holy right to murder hope
> And water ignorance with human blood?
>
> From what high universe-dividing power
> Draw'st thou thy wondrous, ripe brutality?
>
> O horrible ... Thou God who seest these things
> Help us to blot this terror from the earth.

... No, I see it is *To the Czar,** after all. But there are those who would say it fits me — and rather snugly, too. "Ripe brutality." They would say the Czar's isn't ripe yet, but that mine is; and not merely ripe but rotten. Nothing could keep them from saying that;

* Louise Morgan Sill, in *Harper's Weekly.*

they would think it smart. "This terror." Let the Czar keep that name; I am supplied. This long time I have been "the monster"; that was their favorite — the monster of crime. But now I have a new one. They have found a fossil Dinosaur fifty-seven feet long and sixteen feet high, and set it up in the museum in New York and labeled it "Leopold II." But it is no matter, one does not look for manners in a republic. Um ... that reminds me; I have never been caricatured. Could it be that the corsairs of the pencil could not find an offensive symbol that was big enough and ugly enough to do my reputation justice? [*After reflection*] There is no other way — I will buy the Dinosaur. And suppress it.

[*Rests himself with some more chapter headings. Reads*]

More mutilation of children. (Hands cut off.)

Testimony of American Missionaries.

Evidence of British Missionaries.

It is all the same old thing — tedious repetitions and duplications of shop-worn episodes; mutilations, murders, massacres, and so on, and so on, till one gets drowsy over it. Mr. Morel intrudes at this point, and contributes a comment which he could just as well have kept to himself — and throws in some italics, of course; these people can never get along without italics:

> It is one heartrending story of human misery from beginning to end, and *it is all recent.*

Meaning 1904 and 1905. I do not see how a person can act so. This Morel is a king's subject, and reverence for monarchy should have restrained him from reflecting upon me with that exposure. This Morel is a reformer; a Congo reformer. That sizes *him* up. He publishes a sheet in Liverpool called *The West African Mail,* which is supported by the voluntary contributions of the sap-headed and the soft-hearted; and every week it steams and reeks and festers with up-to-date "Congo atrocities" of the sort detailed in this pile of pamphlets here. I will suppress it. I suppressed a Congo atrocity book there, after it was actually in print; it should not be difficult for me to suppress a newspaper.

[*Studies some photographs of mutilated Negroes, throws them down. Sighs*]

The kodak has been a sore calamity to us. The most powerful enemy indeed. In the early years we had no trouble in getting the press to "expose" the tales of the mutilations as slanders, lies, inventions of busy-body American missionaries and exasperated foreigners who found the "open door" of the Berlin-Congo charter closed against them when they innocently went out there to trade; and by the press's help we got the Christian nations everywhere to turn an irritated and unbelieving ear to those tales and say hard things about the tellers of them. Yes, all things went harmoniously and pleasantly in those good days, and I was looked up to as the benefactor of a down-trodden and friendless people. Then all of a sudden came the crash! That is to say, the incorruptible *kodak* — and all the harmony went to hell! The only witness I have encountered in my long experience that I couldn't bribe. Every Yankee missionary and every interrupted trader sent home and got one; and now — oh, well, the pictures get sneaked around everywhere, in spite of all we can do to ferret them out and suppress them. Ten thousand pulpits and ten thousand presses are saying the good word for me all the time and placidly and convinc-

*The only witness
I couldn't bribe!*

ingly denying the mutilations. Then that trivial little kodak, that a child can carry in its pocket, gets up, uttering never a word, and knocks them dumb!

.... What is this fragment?

[*Reads*]

But enough of trying to tally off his crimes! His list is interminable, we should never get to the end of it. His awful shadow lies across his Congo Free State, and under it an unoffending nation of 15,000,000 is withering away and swiftly succumbing of their miseries. It is a land of graves; it is *The* Land of Graves; it is the Congo Free Graveyard. It is a majestic thought: that is, this ghastliest episode in all human history is the work of *one man alone;* one solitary man; just a single individual — Leopold, King of the Belgians. He is personally and solely responsible for all the myriad crimes that have blackened the history of the Congo State. He is *sole* master there; he is absolute. He could have prevented the crimes by his mere command; he could stop them today with a word. He withholds the word. For his pocket's sake.

It seems strange to see a king destroying a nation and laying waste a country for mere sordid money's sake, and solely and only for that. Lust of conquest is royal; kings have always exercised that stately vice; we are used to it, by old habit we condone it, perceiving a certain dignity in it; but *lust of money — lust of shillings — lust of nickels — lust of dirty coin,* not for the nation's enrichment but for *the king's alone* — this is new. It distinctly revolts us, we cannot seem to reconcile ourselves to it, we resent it, we despise it, we say it is shabby, unkingly, out of character. Being democrats we ought to jeer and jest, we ought to rejoice to see the purple dragged in the dirt, but — well, account for it as we may, we don't. We see this awful king, this pitiless and blood-drenched king, this money-crazy king towering toward the sky in a world-solitude of sordid crime, unfellowed and apart from the human race, sole butcher for personal gain findable in all his caste, ancient or modern, pagan or Christian, proper and legitimate target for the scorn of the lowest and the highest, and the execrations of all who hold in cold esteem the oppressor and the coward; and — well, it is a mystery, but *we do not wish to look;* for he is a king, and it hurts us, it troubles us, by ancient and inherited instinct it shames us to see a king degraded to this aspect, and we shrink from hearing the particulars of how it happened. *We shudder and turn away* when we come upon them in print.

Why, certainly — THAT IS MY PROTECTION. And you will continue to do it. I know the human race.

To Them it must appear
very awful and mysterious ...
                              Joseph Conrad

SUPPLEMENTARY

Written for the 1906 edition by MARK TWAIN

Since the first edition of this pamphlet was issued, the Congo story has entered upon a new chapter. The king's Commission concedes the correctness of the delineation contained in the foregoing pages. It affirms the prevalence of frightful abuses under the king's rule. For eight months the king held back the Report but his commissioners had been too deeply moved by the horrors unfolded before them in their visit to the Congo State and the testimony presented to them had reached the world through other sources. The digest of the report, as forwarded from Brussels to the European and American press, was skillfully edited; and the report itself does its best to gloss over the king's responsibility for the shame; but the story told in the genuine document is essentially as hideous as anything found in the depositions of plain-speaking missionaries. So the facts are clear — indisputable, undisputed. The train of revilers of missionary testimony, whose (roseate) pictures of conditions under the king's rule have beguiled the uninformed, hurries out at the wings and Leopold is left to hold the stage, with the skeleton that refuses longer to stay hidden in his Congo closet.

One thing the report omits to do. It does not brand or judge the system out of which the foul breed of iniquities has sprung — the king's claim to personal ownership of 800,000 square miles of territory, with all their products, and his employment of savage hordes to realize on his claim. Judgment of this policy the Commission holds to be beyond its function. Being thus disqualified for striking at the roots of the enormity, the commissioners propose such superficial reforms as occur to them. And the king hastens to take up with their suggestion by calling to his assistance in the work of reform a new Commission. Of this body of fourteen members all but two are committed by their past record to defense and maintenance of the king's Congo policy.

So ends the king's investigation of himself; doubtless less jubilantly than he had planned, but withal as ineffectively as it was foredoomed to end. One stage is achieved. The next in order is action by the Powers responsible for the existence of the Congo State. The United States is one of these. Such procedure is advocated in petitions to the President and Congress, signed by John Wanamaker, Lyman Abbott, Henry Van Dyke, David Starr Jordan and many other leading citizens. If ever the sisterhood of civilized nations have just occasion to go up to The Hague or some other accessible meeting place, a foreordained hour for their assembling has now struck.

SOME THINGS THE REPORT OF THE KING'S COMMISSION SAYS

Apart from the rough plantations which barely suffice to feed the natives themselves and to supply the stations, all the fruits of the soil are considered as the property of the State or of the concessionaire societies .... It has even been admitted that on the land occupied by them the natives cannot dispose of the produce of the soil except to the extent in which they did so before the constitution of the State.

Each official in charge of a Station, or agent in charge of a factory, claimed from the natives, without asking himself on what grounds, the most divers imposts in labor or in kind, either to satisfy his own needs and those of his Station, or to exploit the riches of the Domaine.... The agents themselves regulated the tax and saw to its collection and had a direct interest in increasing its amount, since they received proportional bonuses on the produce thus collected.

Missionaries, both Catholic and Protestant, whom we heard at Leopoldville, were unanimous in accentuating the general wretchedness existing in the region. One of them said that "this system which compels the natives to feed 3,000 workmen at Leopoldville, will, if continued for another five years, wipe out the population of the district."

Judicial officials have informed us of the sorry consequences of the porterage system; it exhausts the unfortunate people subjected to it, and threatens them with partial destruction.

In the majority of cases the native must go one or two days' march every fortnight, until he arrives at that part of the forest where the rubber vines can be met with in a certain degree of abundance. There the collector passes a number of days in a miserable existence. He has to build himself an improvised shelter which cannot, obviously, replace his hut. He has not the food to which he is accustomed. He is deprived of his wife, exposed to the inclemencies of the weather and the attacks of wild beasts. When once he has collected the rubber he must bring it to the State station, or to that of the Company, and only then can he return to his village where he can (sojourn) for barely more than two or three days because the next demand is upon him. It was barely denied that in the various posts of the A. B. I. R. which we visited, the imprisonment of women hostages, the subjection of the chiefs to servile labor, the humiliations meted out to them, the flogging of rubber collectors, the brutality of the black employees set over the prisoners, were the rule commonly followed.

According to the witnesses, these auxiliaries, especially those stationed in the villages, convert themselves into despots, claiming the women and the food; they kill without pity all those who attempt to resist their whims. The truth of the charges is borne out by a mass of evidence and official reports.

The consequences are often very murderous. And one must not be astonished. If in the course of these delicate operations, whose object it is to seize hostages and to intimidate the natives, constant watch cannot be exercised over the (sanguinary) instincts of the soldiers, when orders to punish are given by superior authority, it is difficult to prevent the expedition from degenerating into massacres, accompanied by pillage and (incendiarism.)

THE UNITED STATES
GOVERNMENT AND THE
CONGO STATE

The International Association of the Congo was recognized by the United States April 22, 1884. Nine months afterward, recognition was secured from Germany and, later, successively from the other European Powers. Two international conferences were held at which the Powers constituted themselves guardians of the people of the Congo territory, the Association binding itself to regard the principles of administration adopted. In both these conferences the United States government prominently participated. The Act of Berlin was not submitted by the President of the United States for ratification by the Senate because its adoption as a whole was thought by him to involve responsibility for support of the territorial claims of rival Powers in the Congo region. The Act of Brussels, with a proviso safeguarding this point, was formally ratified by the

United States. Whether we are without obligation to reach a hand to this expiring people, the intelligent reader will judge for himself.

Stanley saw neither fortress nor flag of any civilization save that of the United States, which he carried along the arterial water course.... The first appeal for recognition and for moral support was naturally and justly made to the government whose flag was first carried across the region. — *Mr. Kasson in North American Review, February, 1886.*

This Government at the outset testified its lively interest in the well-being and future progress of the vast region now committed to your Majesty's wise care, by being the first among the Powers to recognize the flag of the International Association of the Congo is that of a friendly State. — *President Clevelandd to King Leopold, September 11, 1885.*

The recognition by the United States was the birth into new life of the Association, seriously menaced as its existence was by opposing interests and ambitions. — *Mr. Stanley, The Congo, vol. I, Page 383.*

He (the President of the United States) desires to see in the delimitation of the region which shall be subjected to this beneficent rule (of the International Association of the Congo) the widest expansion consistent with the just territorial rights of other governments. — *Address of Mr. Kasson, U.S. Representative at Berlin Conference, 1884.*

So marked was the acceptance by the Berlin Conference of the views presented on the part of the United States that Herr von Bunsen, reviewing the action of the Conference, assigns after Germany the first place of influence in the Conference to the United States. — *Mr. Kasson in North American Review, February, 1886.*

In sending a representative to this Assembly, the Government of the U. S. has wished to show the great interest and deep sympathy it feels in the great work of philanthropy which the Conference seeks to realize. Our country must feel beyond all others an immense interest in the work of this Assembly. — *Mr. Terrell, U. S. Representative at Brussels Conference, 1st session, November 19, 1889.*

Mr. Terrell informs the Conference that he has been authorized by this Government to sign the General Act adopted by the Conference.

The President says that the U. S. Minister's communication will be received by the Conference with extreme satisfaction. — *Records of Brussels Conference, June 28, 1890.*

Claiming, as at Berlin, to speak in the name of Almighty God, the signatories (at Brussels) declared themselves to be "equally animated by the firm intention of putting an end to the crimes and devastations engendered by the traffic in African slaves, of protecting effectually the aboriginal populations and of ensuring the benefits of peace and civilization." — *Civilization in Congoland, H. R. Fox Bourne.*

The President continues to hope that the Government of the U. S., which was the first to recognize the Congo Free State, will not be one of the last to give it the assistance of which it may stand in need. — *Remarks of Belgian President of Brussels Conference, session May 14 1890.*

OUGHT KING LEOPOLD TO BE HANGED?*

INTERVIEW BY MR. W. T. STEAD WITH THE
REV. JOHN H. HARRIS, BARINGA, CONGO
STATE, IN THE ENGLISH REVIEW OF REVIEWS
FOR SEPTEMBER, 1905.

For the somewhat startling suggestion in the heading of this interview, the missionary interviewed is in no way responsible. The credit of it, or, if you like, the discredit, belongs entirely to the editor of the *Review*, who, without dogmatism, wishes to pose the question as a matter for serious discussion. Since Charles I's head was cut off, opposite Whitehall, nearly two hundred and fifty years ago, the sanctity which doth hedge about a king has been held in slight and scant regard by the Puritans and their descendants. Hence there is nothing antecedently shocking or outrageous in the discussion of the question whether the acts of any Sovereign are such as to justify the calling in of the services of the

---

* The above article which came to hand as the foregoing was in press is commended to the king and to readers of his Soliloquy. — M. T.

87

public executioner. If is not, of course, for a journalist to pronounce judgment, but no function of the public writer is so imperative as that of calling attention to great wrongs, and no duty is more imperious than that of insisting that no rank or station should be allowed to shield from justice the real criminal when he is once discovered.

The controversy between the Congo Reform Association and the Emperor of the Congo has now arrived at a stage in which it is necessary to take a further step towards the redress of unspeakable wrongs and the punishment of no less unspeakable criminals. The Rev. J. H. Harris, an English missionary, has lived for the last seven years in that region of Central Africa — the Upper Congo — which King Leopold has made over to one of his vampire groups of financial associates (known as the A. B. I. R. Society) on the strictly business basis of a half share in the profits wrung from the blood and misery of the natives. He has now returned to England, and last month he called at Mowbray House to tell me the latest from the Congo. Mr. Harris is a young man in a dangerous state of volcanic fury, and no wonder. After living for seven years face to face with the devastations of the vampire State, it is impossible to deny that he does well to be angry. When he began, as is the wont of those who have emerged from the depths, to detail horrifying stories of murder, the outrage and torture of women, the mutilation of children, and the whole infernal category of horrors, served up with the background of cannibalism, sometimes voluntary and sometimes, incredible though it seems, enforced by the orders of the officers, I cut him short, and said: —

"Dear Mr. Harris, as in Oriental despatches the India Office translator abbreviates the first page of the letter into two words 'after compliments,' or 'a. c.,' so let us abbreviate our conversation about the Congo by the two words 'after atrocities,' or 'a. a.' They are so invariable and so monotonous, as Lord Percy remarked in the House the other day, that it is unnecessary to insist upon them. There is no longer any dispute in the mind of any reasonable person as to what is going on in the Congo. It is the economical exploitation of half a continent carried on by the use of armed force wielded by officials the aim-all and be-all of whose existence is to extort the maximum amount of rubber in the shortest possible time in order to pay the largest possible dividend to the holders of shares in the concessions."

"Well," said Mr. Harris reluctantly, for he is so accustomed to speaking to persons who require to be told the whole dismal tale from A to Z, "what is it you want to know?"

"I want to know," I said, "whether you consider the time is ripe for summoning King Leopold before the bar of an international tribunal to answer for the crimes perpetrated under his orders and in his interest in the Congo State."

Mr. Harris paused for a moment, and then said: — "That depends upon the action which the king takes upon the report of the Commission, which is now in his hands."

"Is that report published?"

"No," said Mr. Harris; "and it is a question whether it will ever be published. Greatly to our surprise, the Commission, which every one expected would be a mere blind whose appointment was intended to throw dust in the eyes of the public, turned out to be composed of highly respectable persons who heard the evidence most impartially, refused no *bona fide* testimony produced by trustworthy witnesses, and were overwhelmed by the multitudinous horrors brought before them, and who, we feel, *must* have arrived at conclusions which necessitate an entire revolution in the administration of the Congo."

"Are you quite sure, Mr. Harris, that this is so?"

"Yes," said Mr. Harris, "quite sure. The Commission impressed us all in the Congo very favorably. Some of its members seemed to us admirable specimens of public-spirited, independent statesmen. They realized that they were acting in judicial capacity; they knew that the eyes of Europe were upon them, and, instead of making their inquiry a farce, they made it a reality, and their conclusions must be, I feel sure, so damning to the State, that if King Leopold were to take no action but to allow the whole infernal business to proceed unchecked, any international tribunal which had powers of a criminal court, would upon the evidence of the Commission alone, send those responsible to the gallows."

"Unfortunately," I said, "at present The Hague Tribunal is not armed with the powers of an international assize court, nor is it qualified to place offenders, crowned or otherwise, in the dock. But don't you think that in the evolution of society the constitution of such a criminal court is a necessity?"

"It would be a great convenience at present," said Mr. Harris; "nor would you need one atom of evidence beyond the report of the Commission to justify the hanging of whoever is responsible for the existence and continuance of such abominations."

"Has anybody seen the text of the report?" I asked.

"As the Commission returned to Brussels in March, some of the contents of that report are an open secret. A great deal of the evidence has been published by the Congo Reform Association. In the Congo the Commissioners admitted two things: first, that the evidence was overwhelming as to the existence of the evils which had hitherto been denied, and secondly, that they vindicated the character of the missionaries. They discovered, as anyone will who goes to that country, that it is the missionaries, and the missionaries alone, who constitute the permanent European element. The Congo State officials come out ignorant of the language, knowing nothing of the country, and with no other sense of their duties beyond that of supporting the concession companies in extorting rubber. They are like men who are dumb and deaf and blind, nor do they wish to be otherwise. In two or three years they

vanish, giving place to other migrants as ignorant as themselves, whereas the missionaries
remain on the spot year after year; they are
in personal touch with the people, whose language they speak, whose customs they respect, and whose lives they endeavor to defend to the best of their ability."

"But, Mr. Harris," I remarked, "was there
not a certain Mr. Grenfell, a Baptist Missionary, who has been all these years a convinced
upholder of the Congo State?"

"'Twas true," said Mr. Harris, "and pity 'tis
'twas true; but 'tis no longer true. Mr. Grenfell has had his eyes opened at last, and he
has now taken his place among those who are
convinced. He could no longer resist the
overwhelming evidence that has been
brought against the Congo Administration."*

"Was the nature of the Commissioners' report," I resumed, "made known to the officials of the State before they left the Congo?"

"To the head officials — yes," said Mr. Harris.

"With what result?"

"In the case of the highest official in the
Congo, the man who corresponds in Africa
to Lord Curzon in India, no sooner was he

* Mr. Grenfell's station is in the Lower Congo, a section remote
from the vast rubber areas of the interior.

placed in possession of the conclusions of the Commission than the appalling significance of their indictment convinced him that the game was up, and he went into his room and cut his throat.

"I was amazed upon returning to Europe to find how little the significance of this suicide was appreciated. A paragraph in the newspaper announced the suicide of a Congo official. None of those who read that paragraph could realize the fact that that suicide had the same significance to the Congo that the suicide, let us say, of Lord Milner would have had if it had taken place immediately on receiving the conclusions of a Royal Commission sent out to report upon his administration in South Africa."

"Well, if that be so, Mr. Harris," I said, "and the Governor-General cuts his throat rather than face the ordeal and disgrace of the exposure, I am almost beginning to hope that we may see King Leopold in the dock at The Hague, after all."

"I will comment upon that," Mr. Harris said, "by quoting you Mrs. Sheldon's remark made before myself, and my colleagues, Messrs. Bond, Ellery, Ruskin, Walbaum and Whiteside, on May 19th last year, when, in answer to our question, 'Why should King

Leopold be afraid of submitting his case to The Hague tribunal?' Mrs. Sheldon answered, 'Men do not go to the gallows and put their heads in a noose if they can avoid it.'"